G. P. PUTNAM'S SONS
A division of Penguin Young Readers Group.
Published by The Penguin Group.
Penguin Group (USA) Inc., 375 Hudson Street, New York, NY 10014, U.S.A.
Penguin Group (Canada), 90 Eglinton Avenue East, Suite 700, Toronto, Ontario, Canada M4P 2Y3
(a division of Pearson Penguin Canada Inc.).
Penguin Books Ltd, 80 Strand, London WC2R 0RL, England.
Penguin Ireland, 25 St. Stephen's Green, Dublin 2, Ireland (a division of Penguin Books Ltd.).
Penguin Group (Australia), 250 Camberwell Road, Camberwell, Victoria 3124, Australia
(a division of Pearson Australia Group Pty Ltd).
Penguin Books India Pvt Ltd, 11 Community Centre, Panchsheel Park, New Delhi - 110 017, India.
Penguin Group (NZ), Cnr Airborne and Rosedale Roads, Albany, Auckland 1310, New Zealand
(a division of Pearson New Zealand Ltd).
Penguin Books (South Africa) (Pty) Ltd, 24 Sturdee Avenue, Rosebank, Johannesburg 2196, South Africa.
Penguin Books Ltd, Registered Offices: 80 Strand, London WC2R 0RL, England.

First American Edition published in 2007 by G. P. Putnam's Sons, a division of Penguin Young Readers Group,
345 Hudson Street, New York, NY 10014. G. P. Putnam's Sons, Reg. U.S. Pat. & Tm. Off.
First published by Lion Hudson plc in 2006. This edition published under license from Lion Hudson plc.
Published simultaneously in Canada. Manufactured in China by South China Printing Co. Ltd.
Design by Katrina Damkoehler.
Text set in Old Claude.

Library of Congress Cataloging-in-Publication Data
Hartman, Bob, 1955–
Dinner in the lions' den / Bob Hartman ; illustrated by Tim Raglin. — 1st American ed.
p. cm.   1. Daniel (Biblical figure)—Juvenile literature.
2. Bible stories, English—O.T. Daniel. I. Raglin, Tim. II. Title.
BS580.D2H27 2007   224'.509505—dc22   2006011930

ISBN 978-0-399-24674-6
1 2 3 4 5 6 7 8 9 10
First Impression

DINNER IN THE LIONS' DEN

BOB HARTMAN · TIM RAGLIN

G. P. PUTNAM'S SONS

KING DARIUS did not want to throw his friend Daniel to the lions. But Daniel's enemies had tricked the king into making a new law . . .

and Daniel had broken that law by praying to his God.

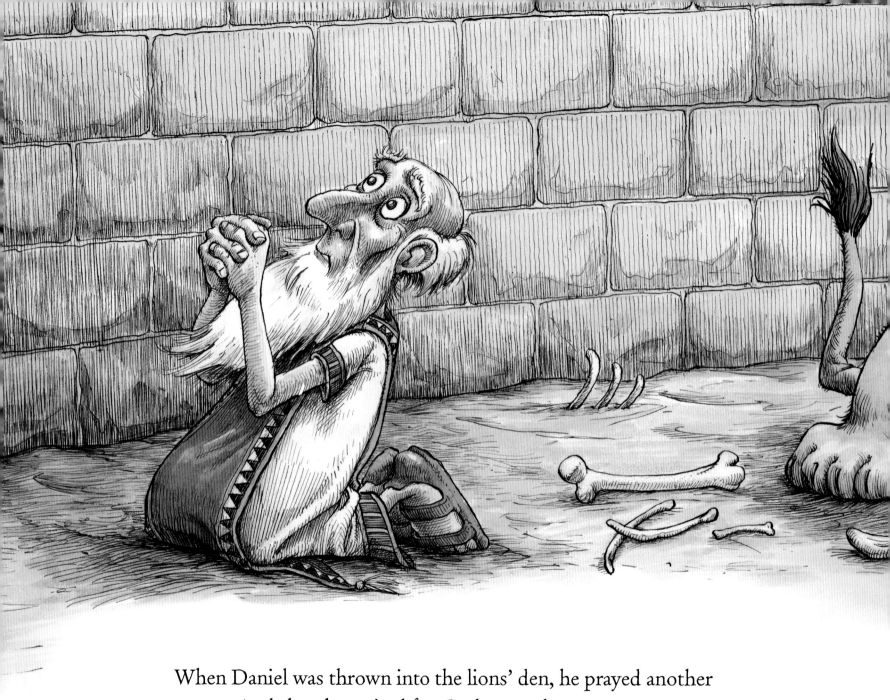

When Daniel was thrown into the lions' den, he prayed another prayer. And then he waited for God to send an answer.

There were four lions in the lions' den.
A father lion. A mother lion. And two tumbling lion cubs.

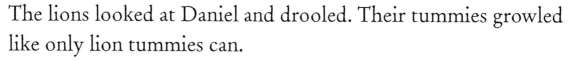

The lions looked at Daniel and drooled. Their tummies growled like only lion tummies can.

"He's skinny and scrawny and old," said Father Lion.

"He'll be tough—but tasty!" said Mother Lion.
"There'll be yummy drumsticks!" said one of the lion cubs.

Suddenly, something like a curtain opened up between heaven and earth. God had heard Daniel's prayer, and God's answer had arrived!

God's answer was an angel. A great big angel who was good with lions!

"It's not time for you to eat yet!" said the angel.

"Oh?" growled Father Lion. "THEN WHAT TIME IS IT, MR. ANGEL?"

The angel smiled. "It's scratching time!" he said.

First the angel scratched behind Father Lion's ears.

Then he scratched Mother Lion.

And last of all he tickled the tumbling lion cubs.

And those chunky fingers felt so good that the lions forgot all about Daniel.

But then one of the lions' tummies growled again. Father Lion glared at Daniel and drooled.
"WHAT TIME IS IT NOW, MR. ANGEL?" he asked.

The angel answered quickly,

"It's belly-rubbing time, of course!"

"Me first!" mewed one of the cubs.
"You were first the last time!" complained the other.
"Everyone will have a turn!" said the angel.

And the next minute, all the lions were
on the floor—wrestling and belly-rubbing
and playing lion games. And the big
angel was playing hardest of all!

At last the lions collapsed on the floor of the den.
Father Lion yawned. "WHAT TIME IS IT NOW, MR. ANGEL?"
"It's sleeping time." The angel yawned.

The lions curled up like house cats in front of the fire.
Soon they were fast asleep.

The next morning, King Darius called down into the den: "Daniel, Daniel . . . Are you still alive, Daniel? Has your God answered your prayers?"

"Yes, Your Majesty!" Daniel called back. "He sent an angel to shut the lions' mouths."

King Darius was delighted. He told his servants to pull Daniel out of the den.

And then he told them to put Daniel's enemies down there in his place!

The lions stood up and stared at Daniel's enemies. Now that the lions were wide awake, they were hungry.

"Good-bye!" said the angel as he pulled aside the curtain between heaven and earth. "I have to get going."

"Wait!" called Father Lion. "I have just one more question.
WHAT TIME IS IT NOW, MR. ANGEL?"

The angel looked at Daniel's enemies,
grinned a wide grin, and said,
"What time is it now?

It's dinnertime!"